JACKSON MAKES HIS MOVE

Story and Pictures by
ANDREW GLASS

FREDERICK WARNE
New York   London

J
G

Frederick Warne & Co., Inc.
New York, New York

Library of Congress Cataloging in Publication Data

Glass, Andrew.
Jackson makes his move.
Summary: An artist searches for new subjects
which would fill his paintings with excitement
and make them come alive.
[1. Painting—Fiction.   2. Artists—Fiction]
I. Title.
PZ7.G48115Jac   [E]   81-15957
ISBN 0-7232-6207-1   AACR2

Printed in the U.S.A. by Princeton Polychrome Press
Typography by Kathleen Westray

86 85 84 83 82 1 2 3 4 5

For my mother,
and with special thanks
to Meredith for all her
help and encouragement.

Jackson was an artist. He painted pictures of trees and streams and wide, blue skies.

He painted portraits of friends and relatives.

He painted portraits of himself.

Everyone loved his pictures — except Jackson.

Once Jackson had loved his pictures too, but little by little he had come to feel that something was missing from his work.

He wasn't satisfied with painting trees anymore. He wanted to paint wind in the trees.

"I wish there was a way to paint the wind," he said, putting down his brushes.

"And the sky is always changing color," Jackson thought, looking up at the sky for a long time.

"How can I paint something that keeps changing?"

It wasn't enough for Jackson that he could draw something perfectly and paint it exactly the color it seemed. "It isn't enough anymore," Jackson thought. "I want to capture the *feeling*."

Jackson wore out his brushes looking for a way to capture feeling. But the skies he painted didn't change, the streams didn't flow, and the trees were only trees. And his portraits were simply not quite right.

"Not quite right is all wrong," Jackson thought.

Finally Jackson packed up his easel and went to see his friend Crackers.

"What's missing?" he asked Crackers. "Why don't my pictures make me happy anymore?"

Crackers spread Jackson's paintings out on the grass and looked at every one.

"They are beautiful," she said, "but they just don't feel new."

"Maybe you need something new to paint," Crackers went on, helping Jackson pack up his paintings. "I think an artist has to make the world seem new again."

Jackson sighed and Crackers patted him on the shoulder. "Start fresh," she exclaimed. "Go someplace you've never been before. The world is big! Paint something that you're truly seeing for the first time!"

"Like what?" asked Jackson, picking up his easel.

"No one can tell an artist what to paint," Crackers said. "When you find what you're looking for, you'll feel it."

Jackson knew she was right. He left on the next train.

He watched the hills and trees flash by his window. Soon they were left far behind.

After many hours he saw tall gray buildings in the distance. Their windows glistened with the colors of the sky.

"I'll paint them," Jackson thought.

The train stopped and Jackson got out.
He was dazzled by the crowded city sidewalks.

"I'll use bright colors to paint the rushing crowds," Jackson said to himself.

"And I'll capture the feeling of impatient drivers in their flashy cars."

He wandered up and down wide busy streets, and he began to feel alone in the big city.

"Got a dime, mister, for a cup of coffee?" squeaked a shabby little character with a wise-guy grin. Jackson took a chance and smiled. "Sure," he said. "This city can be lonely and I could use a friend." "It just so happens that I could use one myself," the little fellow replied. "My name is Sloppy Joe and I'll be your friend!"

Jackson felt much better. They went to a diner and ordered two cups of coffee.

"I'm starting fresh," Jackson told Sloppy Joe as they sipped their coffee. "I'm going to paint this city like it's never been painted before."

Sloppy Joe rolled his eyes. "You'll need a lot of paint." "I mean paint pictures," Jackson said, laughing. "I'm going to paint pictures of cars and rushing crowds and traffic jams and wide lonely streets." Sloppy Joe thought this over. "I'll help you," he offered.

Before long they found a big place to work, and Jackson began to paint. He worked very hard, day after day.

He painted pictures of cars and crowds and huge gray buildings. They looked right.

But they still didn't feel right. "This is a nice painting," Jackson said, holding one up. "But where's the excitement? It's a good picture of the city, but it's still just a picture."

Sloppy Joe looked at the painting too. "Maybe it's not what you're painting," he said thoughtfully, "but how you're painting it. Maybe you haven't put enough of yourself into it."

"How could I put more of myself into it?" Jackson asked crossly. "I'd have to climb right inside the picture."

Suddenly Jackson's eyes lit up.
"Climb inside the picture,"
he whispered to himself.

Then he said it again so loud
that he was almost shouting —
"Inside the picture!"

"Sloppy Joe," he shouted. "I've been standing outside my paintings. I have to get inside them somehow. I know what to do now. I'll paint inside out. I'll put myself into the paintings and paint my own feelings. I'll make my paintings bigger and paint them faster — as fast as feelings are."

"I'll fill my paintings up with life!"

Jackson went to
work directing paint
around the canvas.
Like a traffic cop
at an intersection, he
kept the paint moving.
He used his biggest brushes.
One bright color flowed
smoothly through another.

Jackson lost himself in the swirling and dripping, the splashing and the rubbing.

"What are you doing?" cried Sloppy Joe, coming in from the store with more paint. "Look at this mess!"

"It's like being lost on a crowded street of feelings," Jackson answered without slowing down. "I have to paint my way out."

After a long time Jackson stepped back. He looked carefully at the swirling colors.

And with one last splash of green for home, the painting
was finished.

It looked right.

It felt right too.

It felt great. It wasn't a picture of a certain place, or a picture of any special thing. It wasn't a portrait. It was a painting filled with feelings.

Feelings were woven into the jumble of Jackson's brush strokes. The impatient splatters and splashes of flashy cars swirled through the smooth bright colors of the rushing crowd.

A pale lonely feeling glowed here and there through the sparkling excitement on top.

It was big and bright and filled with life. "What do you think?" Jackson asked Sloppy Joe, his voice trembling with excitement.

"Are you sure it's not upside down?" Sloppy Joe replied.

But he was smiling because he could feel the excitement too. Even upside down, Jackson's painting looked wonderfully alive.

Jackson still works in the city. He paints paintings that are huge and alive with color. They fill his studio like endless windows reflecting the changing colors of the sky.

Still, he is not always happy because each painting is a search for just the right feeling.

Sometimes he finds it,
and sometimes he doesn't.